Superphonics *Storybooks* will help your child to learn to read using Ruth Miskin's highly effective phonic method. Each story is fun to read and has been carefully written to include po and spellings.

The Storybooks are graded so you progress with confidence from easy words to harder ones. There are four levels - Blue (the easiest), Green, Purple and Turquoise (the hardest). Each level is linked to one of the core *Superphonics* Books.

ISBN: 978 0 340 79574 3

Text copyright © 2001 Ruth Miskin
Illustrations copyright © 2001 Michael Reid

Editorial by Gill Munton
Design by Sarah Borny

The rights of Ruth Miskin and Michael Reid to be identified as the author and illustrator of this Work have been asserted by them in accordance with the Copyright, Designs and Patents Act 1988.

First published in Great Britain 2001

10 9 8 7 6 5 4 3

First published in 2001 by Hodder Children's Books,
a division of Hachette Children's Books,
338 Euston Road, London NW1 3BH
An Hachette UK Company. www.hachette.co.uk

Printed and bound in China by WKT Company Ltd.

A CIP record is registered by and held at the British Library.

Target words

This Turquoise Storybook focuses on the following sounds:

ow as in **town**

ou as in **pound**

These target words are featured in the book:

bow	howled	about
brown	howling	astounding
clown	Kingsdown	clouds
cow	now	crouched
crowd	ow	found
crown	owl	house
down	power	loud
eyebrows	prowled	mountain
frowned	scowled	mouse
gown	towel	mouth
growled	town	ouch
growling	wow	out
how		outer

outfit	round	sounds
outfits	shouted	
pounds	shouting	

(Words containing sounds and spellings practised in the Blue, Green and Purple Storybooks and the other Turquoise Storybooks have been used in the story, too.)

Other words

Also included are some common words (e.g. **she**, **what**) which your child will be learning in his or her first few years at school.

A few other words have been used to help the story to flow.

Reading the book

1 Make sure you and your child are sitting in a quiet, comfortable place.

2 Tell him or her a little about the story, without giving too much away:

This is a story about getting ready for a fancy dress party. Sam doesn't have an outfit - until he has a brilliant idea!

This will give your child a mental picture; having a context for a story makes it easier to read the words.

3 Read the target words (above) together. This will mean that you can both enjoy the story without having to spend too much time working out the words. Help your child to sound out each word (e.g. **c-l-ow-n**) before saying the whole word.

4 Let your child read the story aloud. Help him or her with any difficult words and discuss the story as you go along. Stop now and again to ask your child to predict what will happen next. This will help you to see whether he or she has understood what has happened so far.

Above all, enjoy the story, and praise your child's reading!

Ruth Miskin's Superphonics

Turquoise Storybook

Mouse Power!

by **Ruth Miskin**

Illustrated by **Michael Reid**

Hodder
Children's
Books

a division of Hachette Children's Books

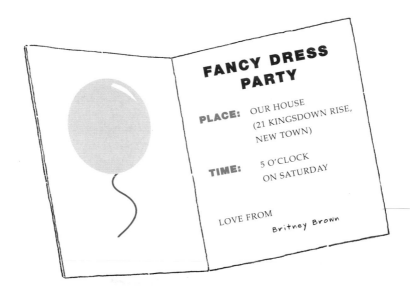

FANCY DRESS PARTY

PLACE: OUR HOUSE
(21 KINGSDOWN RISE, NEW TOWN)

TIME: 5 O'CLOCK
ON SATURDAY

LOVE FROM
Britney Brown

"Wow!" said James.

"A fancy dress party!

Can we go, Mum?"

Mum frowned.

"We must find you all
some fancy dress outfits," she said.

"I've got three pounds!" shouted Sam.
"Let's go into town and get them!"

"I think we've got some outfits
down in the basement," said Mum.

"But these outfits are really old!"

said James. "They're no good now!"

"How about this cow outfit?" said Mum.

"I don't think so!" said James.

"I'm not going out dressed as a cow!"

"I could make it into a gorilla outfit,"

said Mum.

"How could you do that?"

said James.

Mum cut out some big hands and feet.

She stuck them on the cow outfit.

Then she found some bits of brown wool,

and stuck those on as well.

"Now, try it on, James," she said.

"I'll paint a gorilla face on you."

"You don't need to do that!" shouted Sam.

"He looks like a gorilla NOW!"

James crouched down in the gorilla outfit.

He scowled with his gorilla eyebrows,
and made loud "OW! OW! OW!" sounds.

"WOW!" shouted Rebecca.

Sam frowned.

"But what can I be?" he growled.

"You can be a mouse!" said Mum.

"Look at this mouse outfit!"

"I don't want to be a mouse!" said Sam.

"Well, how about a king?" said Mum.

"Here's that crown from the school play!
You can be a king with a crown!"

"I've never seen a king in a dressing gown!"
said Rebecca.

"I didn't want to be a king, anyway,"
growled Sam.

"Now, how about you, Rebecca?" said Mum.

"How about this clown outfit?

Try it on, and bow to the crowd!"

"I don't think so!" said Rebecca.

"I'm not going out dressed as a clown!"

"I could make it into a dragon outfit,"

said Mum.

"How could you do that?" said Rebecca.

Mum found some thick card.
She cut out some brown spikes,
and stuck them to the back
of the clown outfit.

She made a dragon mask.

"Now, try it on, Rebecca," she said.
"I'll stick some cotton wool on to
your mouth."

OUCH!

Rebecca prowled round her magic mountain
in the dragon outfit.

She puffed big clouds of smoke
from her dragon mouth.

"WOW!" shouted James.

Sam scowled.

"BUT WHAT CAN **I** BE?" he howled.

"How about an owl?" said Mum.

"Look, you can wear

this old brown towel.

You can be a wise old owl!"

"I've never seen an owl in a dressing gown!"

said James.

"And an old towel!" said Rebecca.

"I didn't want to be an owl anyway,"

howled Sam.

And he went on howling.

Howling and growling, and shouting,

until Mum said, "Come on, Sam.

Time for bed. We'll make your outfit

in the morning."

"Where's Sam?" said Dad.

"In bed," said James.

"Because he was howling and growling,"

said Rebecca.

In the morning, Dad came in from the shed.

"Look what I've found, Sam!" he said.

"Put this helmet on your head.

Put these straps round your arms.

You can be a spaceman!"

Sam looked at himself
in the spaceman's outfit.
He frowned.

Then he went down
to the basement.

On Saturday, they got ready
to go to the party.

James put on his gorilla outfit.

He crouched down,
and scowled with his gorilla eyebrows.

He made loud "OW! OW! OW!" sounds.

"WOW!" shouted Rebecca.

Rebecca put on her dragon outfit.

She prowled round her magic mountain.

She puffed big clouds of smoke
from her dragon mouth.

"WOW!" shouted James.

And then:

"WOW!" they both shouted.

"Look at Sam!"

"I'm not a spaceman!" shouted Sam.

"I'm a space MOUSE!

A mouse – from outer space!"

"Astounding!" said Dad.

"Hooray for mouse power!"

And they all went to the party –

a gorilla,

a dragon

– and a little

space mouse!